# By the Dawn's Early Light

by KAREN ACKERMAN

illustrated by CATHERINE STOCK

Atheneum Books for Young Readers

*For Carly and Daniel,*
*and with thanks to David Ray*
—K.A.

*For Ily*
—C.S.

At six o'clock, just when we're helping Nana set the table for supper, Mom is getting ready to catch the bus for work. Josh scowls as he puts the knives and forks by the plates. "I always do knives and forks!" he whines as Mom rushes out the door, but he does it anyway.

Mom works in a factory from seven at night to three in the morning. It's called the "graveyard shift." People who work then run places that stay open when everything else is closed, like hospitals, fire departments, and factories. The pay is good, Mom says, and we know she needs the money.

By the time we sit down to a supper of Nana's meat loaf, Mom is waiting in line at the factory door to punch her time card. When the shift whistle blows, she gets a work apron and a set of earplugs so the roar of the machines won't ruin her hearing.

After supper I help dry the dishes. Josh hands the plates and cups to Nana when I'm done drying, and she puts them in the cupboard. Then we sit at the kitchen table, and Josh draws with his new colored markers. "Don't you have homework, Rachel?" Nana asks me.

By then Mom is working the machine that makes creases in the flattened cardboard boxes moving on a conveyor belt. Down the line her friend Lacey puts the boxes in tall stacks to be tied and shipped. Her other friend Bess puts the shipping labels on.

I find my notebooks and get down to work while
Nana peeks over my shoulder. Every now and then
she reads one of the answers on my homework paper
and murmurs, "That's right, honey!" or "Try again,
sweetheart." Later she puts two cups of milk and a
dish of cookies on the table.

It's coffee-break time for Mom when a bell rings once. She turns off the machine and gets her coin purse. Mom, Lacey, and Bess walk through the factory to the cafeteria, where they sit and talk and maybe play a hand or two of rummy. When the bell rings again, it's back to work.

Soon it's time to take our baths and put on our pj's. We brush our teeth, give Nana a kiss, and crawl into our beds. Nana reads a story to Josh, who can't fall asleep without one, then goes downstairs to watch the TV news.

When our hall clock chimes eleven, Mom hears the lunch bell ring twice. She shuts down the machine and heads for the cafeteria with Bess and Lacey for a whole half hour. Her favorite dish is the "low cal" tomato stuffed with tuna salad and extra oyster crackers. She stops in the ladies' lounge to brush her teeth before she goes back to work again.

Our house is silent and dark, and even Nana is fast asleep when Mom gets her last coffee break at 1:00 A.M.

Then, before the dawn's early light, the shift whistle blows. Mom punches her time card and catches the bus for home. At four in the morning most people are still tucked under the covers, in the middle of dreams. But some people are just coming home, like Mom.

She unlocks the front door and closes it quietly, then slips off her shoes and hangs her coat in the closet. While the streetlamps hum and cast a cool white light, she sits in a chair, rubs her toes, and puts up her feet for "good circulation."

Sometimes I wake up when I hear Mom unlock the front door. Slipping out of bed, I tiptoe to Josh's room and wake him up. "Mom's home," I whisper, and he rubs his eyes. I help him put on his robe with the matching slippers.

"What are you two doing up?" Mom asks when she sees us looking down from the top of the stairway. She smiles and opens her arms wide, and we come down the stairs. Kneeling on each side of her chair, we trade hugs.

Mom smells like the cardboard boxes she works with at the factory, a woodsy scent of paper and glue, and she looks at each of our faces closely.

"Who's hungry?" Mom asks, and we follow her into the kitchen. She cuts up oranges to make fresh-squeezed juice, and the smell of orange peels fills the kitchen.

We both have big bowls of cereal, since we won't have to get ready for school for another hour and a half. For Mom it's a supper of Nana's leftover meat loaf and gravy heated up in the oven.

After our cereal and juice we help Mom rinse out the bowls, and then we all go back into the living room and sit on the sofa. We lay our heads in Mom's lap and tuck our slippered feet under the folds of our robes. Beneath my head I can feel Mom's legs tremble a little from standing all the time at work. She runs her fingers through our hair.

"What did you do while I was at work?" Mom asks, and we take turns telling her. Josh shows her what he drew with the colored markers, and I show her my homework paper. Mom looks at it very carefully, finds a few mistakes, and helps me fix them.

"Did Nana work when you were little?" I ask.

Mom shakes her head. "Things were different then, Rachel, and Grandpa was there," she answers. I know it's probably hard for Mom to pay for everything, and I feel kind of sorry I asked.

"Are you two mad at me because I have to work all night?" Mom asks. Her eyes look tired, and shadows show underneath them. We are a little mad because everybody else's parents work during the day, but neither one of us wants to say so.

I shake my head and start to tickle Mom under her arms, hoping she can't see how I really feel. Josh starts to tickle her too, and we get her laughing so hard that she yelps, "I give! I give!" to make us stop.

Suddenly the lamp clicks on in Nana's room.

In a few minutes Nana comes out into the hallway on her way to the bathroom. She looks nearly as tired as Mom does, wearing a sleep hairnet and fuzzy slippers.

"Good morning!" Nana mumbles as she heads toward the bathroom. "I'll get breakfast ready in a few minutes," she adds, closing the bathroom door behind her. She's got the shower going before any of us can say we've already had breakfast.

"I couldn't make it without your Nana," Mom says, softly chuckling to herself. "None of us could!"

The three of us sit together on the sofa and watch the pinkish gold sunrise through the living room window.

Maybe someday Mom will be able to work the same hours as other parents we know. Then the only sound in our house at sunrise will be the sound of us asleep, tucked under the covers, and in the middle of our dreams.

But, for now, at least we can be together by the dawn's early light.

Atheneum Books for Young Readers
An imprint of Simon & Schuster Children's Publishing Division
1230 Avenue of the Americas
New York, New York 10020

First edition
Printed in the United States of America on recycled paper.


10   9   8   7   6   5

The text of this book is set in Aster.
The illustrations are rendered in watercolor.

Library of Congress Cataloging-in-Publication Data

Ackerman, Karen, 1951–
    By the dawn's early light / by Karen Ackerman; illustrated by
Catherine Stock. — 1st ed.
        p.    cm.
    Summary: A young girl and her brother stay with their grandmother
while their mother works at night.
    ISBN 0-689-31788-3
    [1. Single-parent family—Fiction.   2. Mothers—Employment—
Fiction.   3. Grandmothers—Fiction.]   I. Stock, Catherine, ill.
II. Title.
PZ7.A1824By   1994
[E]—dc20                                                92-35633